The Noon Balloon

PaRragon

Bath • New York • Cologne • Melbourne • Delhi
Hong Kong • Shenzhen • Singapore

A girl and boy wished they could fly,
On a magical journey through the sky.

They climbed aboard the Noon Balloon!
It was swift as the wind and round as the moon.

Where would they travel, and what would they do,
Floating through the skies so blue?

Over the treetops and far away,
Over the sea where the mermaids play.

They whooshed along on a galloping breeze,
Sailing above waves and swirling seas.

A land of clover stretched pink and sweet,
They heard bees buzz and songbirds tweet.

A dragonfly flashed up, ready to play,
Then sped ahead to show them the way.

Onward they flew through the bright clear air,
Over valleys and hills, though they knew not where.

"Look!" said the boy, who had spotted a clown.
Then they heard distant cheers from a circus in town.

Six little balloons floated up from below,
They danced in the air as if saying hello.

"Blow away!" called the clown and what else could they do?
They caught the breeze and away they flew.

Where were they going? Would they get there soon?
On through the sky flew the Noon Balloon ...

Then suddenly, the clouds grew dark,
And the little dog began to bark.

Great gold lightning split the sky!
Whirling, swirling, way up high.

The little girl shouted, "Hold on tight!"
They grabbed the ropes with all their might.

The Noon Balloon was rocked and spun!
Then, just like that, out popped the sun.

Biff! And bang! Smoke filled the sky.
Below them, cars went whizzing by.

Shiny buildings, left and right.
The air was thick; the lights were bright.

The city's rhythm, like a drum.
Chug-a-rum, chug-a-rum, chug-a-rum, chug-a-rum.

They left the city far behind
For more exciting things to find!

Now way up high, a bbrrrr and roar!
They saw an airplane dip and soar.

Backward, forward, here and there,
Airplanes, airplanes everywhere!

Where were they going? Would they get there soon?
On through the sky flew the Noon Balloon ...

And then there were no sounds at all,
As the golden sun began to fall.

Past magical gardens of roses and mint,
Where water sparkles and fireflies glint.

The afternoon was deep and warm.
A thin white moon began to form.

The Noon Balloon then stopped and bowed,
Descending softly as a cloud.

They'd reached an unfamiliar land,
An ancient forest, tall and grand.

A secret village; what a sight!
One hundred candles burning bright.

Tiny houses in the trees,
Nestled, snug between the leaves.

They played all night, then played some more
So high above the forest floor.

And when the dawn began to show,
A restless wind began to blow.

They climbed once more into the skies,
While a golden sun began to rise.

They knew where to go, and they'd get there soon.
Back through the sky flew the Noon Balloon.